The Ghost of Charlotte Lighthouse

Sally Valentine

North Country Books • Utica, New York

The Ghost of the Charlotte Lighthouse

ISBN 1-59531-013-4

North Country Books, Inc
311 Turner Street
Utica, New York 13501
www.northcountrybooks.com

This book is dedicated to the teachers of the City School District of Rochester, New York, past, present, and future. Your collective light outshines the world's greatest lighthouses. Only God knows how many ships you have saved from treacherous waters.

Scratch, scratch, scratch . . . . .

Chapter 1

On a cliff overlooking Lake Ontario, the Genesee River, and the port of Rochester, New York, a lonely lighthouse still stood watch. Its windows were boarded up and its roof was leaking. Its face was dirty and its light had long since gone out. Its front door was hidden with brush and its stairs were crumbling. But maybe you wouldn't look so good either if you were 127 years old.

From inside the lighthouse tower came the sound of scratching, but no one was there to hear it. That is, no human ears were there to hear it, because the lighthouse had been abandoned for eighteen years.

* * *

Across town, life was very different. Susan B. Anthony School #27 was vibrating with energy, and there were twenty pairs of ears open to hear Janie cry out.

"Ow! Ow! Ow! Ow!" she yelled as she hobbled from her seat to line up for music class. Everyone in the class laughed, even her best friend, Jeanetta, who quickly covered her mouth and tried to give her a sympathetic glance. Janie couldn't help it if her foot had fallen asleep during English class and was now sending pins

1

and needles up and down her leg. It was a miracle that her whole body hadn't fallen asleep while Mrs. Levine was explaining how a subject and predicate must always agree. What two people ever always agree, thought Janie. But she wouldn't say that to Mrs. Levine.

Mrs. Levine just heaved one of her famous sighs. Everyone agreed that Mrs. Levine was the best sigher at Susan B. Anthony School #27. Her sighs seemed to start at the top of her blond (dyed, everyone said) head, picked up speed as they rolled by the considerable fat around her middle, and dropped like Santa in the chimney with a great crash at the bottom of her size ten feet.

"Okay," said Mrs. Levine. "Let's see if you can walk down the hall quietly. After music class we'll start talking about our new class project based on *Titanic*."

The kids oohed and aahed but managed some semblance of order as they headed out the door. The year was 1999, and *Titanic* was the hottest movie that year. Just about everyone in the fourth grade class had seen it even though it was rated PG-13. This ought to hold their interest at least for a little while, thought Mrs. Levine as she ran straight to the teachers' room for that bagel and coffee she had been thinking about all morning.

Later, Mrs. Levine explained how they would divide up into groups to do research on the *Titanic* and other ships that had sunk. School #27 was a charter school that was based on cooperative learning, and the class was used to studying in groups. That strategy seemed to work, as the school won the prestigious Herman Goldberg Award for academic excellence in its first year of operation. Parents who opted to send their children to #27 did so because of its high academic standards as well as its success at getting students from all different kinds of backgrounds to get along with each other.

Janie and Jeanetta crossed their fingers as Mrs. Levine got ready to read the names of the students in each group. The groups changed for each project, and Janie and Jeanetta had not been in a group together all year. They both held their breaths when Mrs. Levine began to read the lists.

"Group 1 will be Anthony, Bobby, Justina, Debra, and Shakeya." She paused.

"Group 2 will be Donald, Maria, Tomas, Felicia, and Tawanda." She paused again.

"Group 3 will be Janie, Derrick, Reinaldo, Lamar, and...Jeanetta."

Janie barely heard the names of the last group; she was working hard not to seem too pleased. Mrs. Levine might change her mind if she seemed too happy. Teachers were like that.

Jeanetta was happy too, but worried about how they were going to work with the boys in the group. How could anyone cooperate with someone like Derrick, and what if Lamar found out she had a crush on him?

Janie and Jeanetta had been best friends ever since the first day of school in second grade. Janie tripped off the school bus and fell into Jeanetta, who had been walking ahead of her. Unfortunately, Mr. Rodriguez, the bus driver, had dropped them off right next to a mud puddle the size of Lake Ontario. Two boys on the Safety

Patrol picked them up and then gathered their pencils, crayons and other new school supplies. Everything had been scattered all around and was now covered with mud. When Janie saw Jeanetta looking like a hoot owl with muddy rings around her eyes, she started to giggle. When Jeanetta saw Janie spotted with mud like a Dalmatian, she started to giggle. They had been giggling together ever since. The fact that both of their names began with *J* only cinched the friendship, and the fact that their skin was different colors did nothing to hinder it.

Work on the *Titanic* project became everyone's favorite part of the school day. Their first assignment was to come up with a name for their group.

Jeanetta said, "Let's call our group The Mermaids since we're working on an ocean project."

"That's a stupid name," said Derrick. "If you want this group to be named The Mermaids, I'm going to ask to be in another group."

"Having you in another group might be a good idea," said Janie.

Mrs. Levine happened to walk by at that moment and urged them to try harder to cooperate. Reinaldo suggested The Wreckers, but the girls vetoed that idea. They thought about and rejected The Captains, The Sailors, The Pirates, and The Salvagers.

Derrick said, "Let's call our group The Sea Dogs; you girls look like dogs from the sea." Janie and Jeanetta kicked him under the table at the same time.

"Ouch! Mrs. Levine, the girls are kicking me for no reason."

"Maybe Group 3 will need some time inside at recess to think up a name," said Mrs. Levine in her meanest teacher voice. She hadn't earned the nickname, "Mean Levine," for nothing.

"You'd better not get us detention," Reinaldo warned Derrick.

Derrick was about to respond when Lamar jumped up.

"I've got it," he said. "Let's call our group The Starfish."

"Yeah," said Derrick. "I like the name Starfish. Only let's capitalize all the letters in the word star. Even with the girls in our group we can be the stars of this classroom."

"And," said Jeanetta getting into the spirit of the name, "There are five people in our group and five arms on a starfish. It fits perfectly." Jeanetta had an orderly mind and liked things nice and neat.

Reinaldo and Janie nodded in agreement and The STARfish were born.

Chapter 2

The next step in the research project involved taking a walking trip to the Webster Ave. branch of the Rochester Public Library. Mrs. Levine threatened everyone with detention for a week if they didn't behave like "ladies and gentlemen." Detention at PS #27 was a serious thing. The school buses left promptly at 3:25 P.M., and students with detention had to wait until their father or mother could come and pick them up.

"We'll walk down the port side of Central Park, cross over to the starboard side of Goodman Street, and then full steam ahead on Bay Street to Webster Avenue," ordered Mrs. Levine, who had decided to use ship vocabulary for the rest of the school year. Central Park in Rochester was not a true park like in New York City, but just a wide street with a strip of grass running down the middle.

Of course it rained the day of the field trip. However, Mrs. Levine, like most teachers, was ready for any emergency and provided plastic garbage bags as temporary raincoats for those students who were without. It wasn't cool to wear a real raincoat to school, but a plastic bag on certain occasions could definitely be cool.

As they headed out the door and down the port side of Central Park, Mrs. Levine said, "I'm afraid rain goes with Rochester the way cheeseburgers go with McDonald's." Not one to lose a teaching opportunity, she then challenged the students to make their own comparisons. So passersby walking down the street heard the sound of twenty students, three parents, and one teacher saying things like, "Rain goes with Rochester like babies go with diapers, like rings go with Saturn, like Popsicles go with summer, like boys go with B.O." This last comparison was made by Jeanetta and fortunately not heard by Mrs. Levine.

The class had rounded the last corner and was within sight of the library when Janie tripped over an uneven sidewalk, fell down, skinned her knee, and started bleeding. Janie had grown four inches in the last year, all in her legs. The rest of her body had yet to adjust. Mrs. Levine, of course, had planned for such an emergency by bringing her first aid kit. She hustled the group into the library where she attended to Janie's wound saying, "Teachers, like Boy Scouts, must always be prepared."

Ms. Romano, the librarian, read them one of the new books about the *Titanic*, and then sent them off to look through other books and reference materials. When they were out of Ms. Romano's sight, Derrick sneaked up on Janie. He took a worm that he had picked up off the wet sidewalk out of his pocket. He dangled it in front of her eyes and then dropped it into her hair.

"What's the matter, Janie, did you trip over a worm outside?" Derrick sneered.

Janie had no choice but to scream. All of her eighteen classmates ran to see what had happened. They were followed by the three parents, one teacher, two librarians, and all of the other people visiting the library that day. Through gritted teeth Mrs. Levine said, "Only bookworms are allowed in libraries. I'll see you both for detention."

* * *

Detention this time was actually not all bad—at least after the first day when Mrs. Levine made them write letters of apology to Ms. Romano for their childish and rude behavior. Janie wanted to remind Mrs. Levine that children are supposed to behave childishly. However, one look at the scowl on her teacher's face made her think that maybe she should just be quiet and write the letter.

Mr. Washburn, Janie's father, wasn't even mad at her. He told her that it was a good thing to scream if any boy messed with her. On the third and last night of detention they even stopped for ice cream on the way home.

Derrick's mom, Mrs. Davis, was not as nice to Derrick. She punished him again at home by not letting him watch TV or play video games all week. And that was a real punishment. Even worse than the punishment were the lectures about how he was the oldest and had to be the man in the family and set a good example for Louis and Richard, his two younger brothers. It wasn't fair! Nobody had asked him if he wanted to be the oldest in the family, even if he did get to stay up later than his two pesty brothers.

Derrick didn't mean to get into trouble. It was just that his hands or his feet or his lips sometimes did or said things that his mind hadn't had a chance to think about yet. Like last week—he didn't mean to wreck Debra's homework. It was just that the math paper was sticking out of her bookbag, and seemed to be calling him to touch it. The homework ended up ripped and dirty and stuck in one of the holes in the school parking lot's chain link fence. How did that happen? Good thing his mother never found out about that.

Why am I always the one in trouble, he thought, while sulking in his room one night. Of average height and weight, dressed in a T-shirt and jeans, his hair worn short in a buzz cut, Derrick did look like most of the other boys in the classroom. So why was he always in trouble and his friend Lamar never in trouble? Mrs. Levine just doesn't like me, thought Derrick. It must be the glasses. That's the only thing that makes Lamar different from me. She must like Lamar better because he wears glasses and that makes him look smarter.

Chapter 3

Mrs. Levine made Janie and Derrick put their after school time to good use by doing more research on the *Titanic* and then reporting back to the class. They were surprised to learn that there had been six Rochesterians on board the *Titanic*, and three of them had died. She made them pretend to be survivors of the *Titanic* and had the class interview them like reporters for the *Rochester Democrat & Chronicle*. Derrick pretended to be first class passenger, Mr. Jeremiah P. Meriweather, from London. Janie pretended to be steerage class passenger, Elizabeth Morgan, from Liverpool. Derrick made everyone laugh by adding "Pip, Pip, Cheerio" to the end of every answer.

As the weeks went on they built scale models of the *Titanic* and the lifeboats, ate food similar to that served on the *Titanic*, did science experiments with ice and water, and solved related math problems. As this unit was drawing to a close, Mrs. Levine surprised them by saying, "I bet you didn't know that we have had ship-wrecks right here on Lake Ontario."

"Aw, Miz Levine, Lake Ontario ain't no ocean," said Derrick.

"No, Derrick, Lake Ontario isn't an ocean, but the Great Lakes can accommodate ocean going ships. They hold more fresh water than any other lakes in the world. Did you know that if you put all five Great Lakes end to end they would reach from Rochester to Miami, Florida?"

Before she pulled down the classroom's U.S. map Mrs. Levine challenged, "I'll treat anyone who can name all of the Great Lakes to an ice cream sundae at lunch time."

"Well, we know there's Ontario," said Derrick.

"What about Lake Erie and Seneca Lake?" chimed in Reinaldo.

"Lake Erie is one of the Great Lakes. In fact, it's the one that's connected to Lake Ontario by the Niagara River and the Welland Canal," replied Mrs. Levine. "But Seneca is one of the Finger Lakes, not one of the Great Lakes."

"If Seneca is a finger lake then where is its nail?" said Janie under her breath.

Mrs. Levine, with her supersonic hearing, heard her anyway. "The reason some of the other lakes near Rochester are called the Finger Lakes, Janie, is that they are long and narrow and are lined up in a row. From an airplane they look like fingers. The Iroquois Indians, who were the first inhabitants of western New York, described the Finger Lakes as the imprint from God's hand. They're also the ones who named our Lake Ontario. It means great or beautiful lake."

"Let us see the map," said Shekeya.

"Just a minute," said Mrs. Levine. "Let's see if anyone

can come up with another guess first."

"I know," said Jeanetta. "Lake Michigan is one of the Great Lakes."

"How'd you know that?" asked Rodney.

"Easy," replied Jeanetta. "My cousin Tyrone lives in Chicago, and he goes swimming in Lake Michigan."

The class made a few more guesses like Canandaigua Lake, Keuka Lake and Irondequoit Lake. "Well, we're getting farther astray. Canandaigua and Keuka are Finger Lakes and Irondequoit is a bay off of Lake Ontario. Let me show you how my teacher taught me the names of the Great Lakes about 100 years ago." Everyone laughed as she turned to the chalkboard and wrote:

H uron
O ntario
M ichigan
E rie
S uperior

"Hey," said Lamar. "The first letters going down spell homes."

"That's right," said Mrs. Levine. "That's how you can remember the names."

"Is Huron Lake the biggest?" asked Felicia.

"No, Lake Huron is not the largest. Actually Lake Superior is the largest and northernmost on the map," said Mrs. Levine," as she pointed to the classroom map and continued to lead the discussion.

The next day the class, especially the boys, wanted

to know more about the shipwrecks on the Great Lakes. Mrs. Levine said that in 1908 there had been a steamboat, ironically named the *Titania*, which sank right by the Charlotte Pier after colliding with another boat. "Luckily, children, all twenty-one of the passengers survived. But in some ways the Great Lakes are more treacherous than the oceans."

"Do they get icebergs?" yelled out Brian.

"They don't exactly get icebergs," replied Mrs. Levine patiently. "But Lake Erie usually gets totally frozen over in the winter because it's the shallowest of the lakes. In fact, in the spring, a special boat called a cutter goes through the lakes and the connecting canals to break the ice. This way the larger ships can sail safely through."

"If there aren't any icebergs, then what causes shipwrecks on the Great Lakes?" Lamar wanted to know.

"Usually the weather," replied Mrs. Levine. "Strong storms with winds of fifty-two or more knots can create waves that will go over the tops of some of the ships. Also, the tossing and turning in the waves can break apart a ship that might not be strong enough. A ship in the ocean might be able to steer around a storm, but in the Great Lakes there is nowhere else to go. A captain wouldn't have any choice except to ride right into the storm."

"Let's do some research and find out what other things might have caused shipwrecks," said Mrs. Levine. Not wanting to chance another trip to the library so soon, she passed out books and copies of articles related to the shipwrecks. She also allowed one person from each group to do research on the classroom computer.

Mrs. Levine was an old-fashioned teacher who trusted books more than she trusted the Internet. In fact, the only reason she had a computer in her room at all was because the parents and Mr. Coley, the school principal, demanded it.

The kids quickly became involved in the research. The STARfish found out that some ships had been destroyed by funnel clouds called waterspouts. Others ran into trouble because they carried too much cargo. The *Seabird* sank in 1868 because a careless crewman had thrown ashes from the coal furnace off the windward side of the ship. The strong wind blew the ashes right back at the ship, starting a fire.

"How could a ship catch on fire with all that water around to put it out?" wondered Janie aloud. Nobody really knew, so they read some more to find out that the ships were often made of wood and carried cargo like wheat. Wood and wheat were both extremely combustible. Also, the ships didn't have the right equipment to get the lake water to the fires.

"Look at this," yelled out Derrick. "A ship called the *Cornealia E. Windiate* disappeared in 1875 on the way from Milwaukee to Buffalo. No one ever saw it again!"

"Cool!" replied the rest of the group in unison.

"I think those ships that were never heard from again were called Flying Dutchmen," said Jeanetta, who had been quietly reading to herself.

"What else did you read, smartypants?" said Derrick.

"Well, I read that in the twenty years between 1879 and 1899, 6,000 ships were wrecked on the Great

Lakes, and some people think that there's $800,000,000 worth of salvageable stuff still at the bottom of the lakes."

"Whoa," said all the boys together. They were impressed, but didn't want to admit that a girl knew more about shipwrecks than they did.

Chapter 4

On the way home from school that day Reinaldo said to Derrick and Lamar, "I wish we could find some treasures from a ship that sank in Lake Ontario. That would show those girls who knows more about shipwrecks."

"Well," suggested Derrick, "why don't we go to the beach and dig for some? Maybe some gold doubloons will be buried in the sand."

"Yeah, or maybe a dead body even," interjected Reinaldo.

"I bet we can talk my brother Steven into taking us to Durand Eastman Park," chimed in Lamar. The three boys raced the rest of the way home.

"What kind of school project is this?" asked Steven after they were all loaded in his car. "We didn't have no projects like this when I was in school," he continued, sounding like he was forty-nine instead of nineteen. "Besides, this ain't Florida. Who goes to the beach in Rochester in March?" Steven worked the midnight shift at the Mini-Mart on Norton Street and was in charge of Lamar until their mother got home at six o'clock. Steven drove a black Mustang that he had equipped with the "baddest" stereo system around. Normally he wouldn't have wasted his time on the boys, but he was between girlfriends and had some time on his hands. When he saw their pile of shovels, pails, and strainers, Steven almost changed his mind.

"Don't be dirtying up my car with that nasty stuff now. If Mama sees that strainer you took from her kitchen, she's gonna have both our heads." Steven relented when they promised to cover his trunk floor with an old shower curtain they found on a shelf, and they vibrated down the street to the sounds of Puff Daddy screaming through the rolled up windows.

At the lake they ignored the BEACH CLOSED sign and waded, boots and all, into the cold lake water. It wasn't long before Reinaldo yelled out, "I think I found something." The other boys rushed over and used their shovels to help him uncover a silver object that was just barely sticking out of the sand.

"It's a silver spoon," shouted Derrick. "Maybe it's real silver and we'll find a whole set." The spoon was bent and mangled, and looked like it had been in the water a hundred years. Part of a design was faint, but still visible, on the handle.

"Maybe it belonged to a rich lady," said Reinaldo.

"Maybe we'll get a reward and our names in the paper," added Lamar.

They continued digging and sifting, but the only things they turned up in the next hour were an old sneaker, a pink florescent Frisbee that had a chunk missing, and an empty bottle of Coppertone suntan lotion. "Jeez," moaned Derrick. " Don't people know they're not supposed to pollute?"

"Well, at least we have the one spoon," said Reinaldo. "Maybe Mrs. Levine can help us find out where it's from, and we can come back tomorrow and dig farther down the beach."

"Good idea," said Derrick, whose feet were freezing since the water had come over the top of his boots. He didn't want to admit that he was cold, but he was afraid that he had frostbite.

The boys walked as fast as their frozen toes would let them back to Steven, who had never gotten out of the car and had cranked the volume up on his sound system to the earth-moving level. Steven gave them one long look and made them take off boots, socks, and pants before letting them in his back seat.

"You can't make us take our pants off," argued Lamar, but he had no chance of winning against Steven, who replied, "I ain't having my car smell like no dead fish." Steven did agree to crank the heat up to the level of the sound system, but the boys had not yet started to thaw when freezing pellets of rain started pinging on the windshield, almost keeping time to the music.

"Rain goes with Rochester the way Steven goes with rap music," stammered Reinaldo between his still chattering teeth. Derrick and Lamar just nodded, their jaws still too cold to smile. Steven never heard him.

When they arrived home, Lamar ran right up to the bathtub and filled it with hot water. The boys all sat on the edge of the tub and screamed as they plunged their frozen feet into the steaming water, not realizing that this was not the best way to warm up ice cold feet. The screams eventually turned to sighs as they slowly started to thaw out.

"Do you think this is how the water feels in Jamaica?" wondered Lamar. They all laughed while wishing they were anywhere except in Rochester, New York, which has six months of winter, three months of fall, three months of summer, and no spring at all.

Chapter 5

The boys agreed that since Reinaldo had been the one to first find the spoon, he should be the one to take it to school and ask Mrs. Levine about it. The boys, of course, couldn't resist telling about their adventure and bragging about their find on the playground before school. And the girls, of course, couldn't resist "dissing" them. "Who'd want to eat with a dirty, jagged old spoon that smells like fish, anyway?" said Janie.

"Let me look at that pattern again," said Jeanetta, but she barely had time to make out part of what might be a flower design when Derrick snatched the spoon away from her again.

"This may be old and dirty, but we don't want any girls' cooties on it anyway."

At that moment Mrs. Levine's blue Taurus came around the corner, and the kids flew over and stuck the spoon in her face before she could even set one foot out of the car. "Let me take this and study it for a few minutes," said Mrs. Levine as she struggled to get her balance. "Then we'll talk about it after the bell rings."

Mrs. Levine felt like the head juror on the O.J.

Simpson trial as she stood in the classroom to give her verdict. Before she could speak she looked over to where Jeanetta was doodling something on the back of her homework. "What's that you're drawing, Jeanetta?" asked Mrs. Levine. She was stalling while trying to think of the right way to phrase her answer.

"Oh, nothing, Mrs. Levine. It's just that the spoon reminds me of something."

"It reminds me of something too," said Mrs. Levine. "Even though this spoon is scratched and mangled, I think I have eight just like it at home. This is part of a set that Wegmans was giving away as a promotion a few years ago. You got a piece every time you spent $100 in groceries."

"That's why it's familiar," shouted Jeanetta. "Aunt Henrietta has a set just like that." She looked over at Reinaldo, who was looking at the floor. Derrick was slouched down in his desk and Lamar was writing on his sneaker. None of the boys said a word.

Janie hit Derrick on the back. "If I had found the spoon I would have thought it was buried treasure too," she said in a rare display of sympathy.

"At least you had an adventure," agreed Shakeya.

"Let's all go to the beach tonight and look some more," added Donald.

Mrs. Levine was quick to put a stop to that idea, promising a class trip there when the weather got warmer. She concluded with a stern lecture about the dangers of going to the beach when it was closed and no lifeguards were around. Derrick wondered if teachers got extra pay for all the lectures they gave kids. Maybe each lecture was worth $100, he theorized, and if you gave over ten lectures in one week you got a bonus. He decided that this was not the best time to ask Mrs. Levine about that and reluctantly promised, along with the rest of the class, that he would do no more salvaging on his own.

Chapter 6

The next morning Mrs. Levine came in with a new announcement. "I've been thinking," she began. Oh no, thought Janie. When Mrs. Levine starts thinking that means more homework for all of us. She stole a glance at Jeanetta, who seemed to be listening intently to their teacher. That figures, thought Janie; Jeanetta doesn't even mind if we get extra homework.

"I've been thinking," continued Mrs. Levine, "about why Reinaldo, Derrick, and Lamar didn't find any shipwreck treasure in Lake Ontario. It might be because, for years here in Rochester, we've had something to guide ships safely into the harbor. This prevented most of them from getting lost or pummeled on the rocks or beached on the sand bar. Does anyone know what that is?"

"Is it that light on the end of the Charlotte pier?" asked Maria.

"Right now it's the light at the end of the pier. But for years a lighthouse and the lighthouse keeper who lived there guarded the harbor to keep ships and their passengers safe. I've invited my friend Mr. Davidson from the Lighthouse Historical Society to come to talk to us, and he has invited us to come and visit him at the lighthouse."

Mr. Davidson was a tall, thin man with a few strands of white hair on an otherwise bald head. Mrs. Levine said it wasn't polite to ask a grownup his age, but Mr. Davidson didn't seem to mind when Tomas asked. He replied, "I'm seventy-seven years and five months old. I was born in 1920 while my daddy Augustus Davidson was the keeper of the light. My sister Clara and me grew up in the keeper's house. 'Course by then the old lighthouse tower wasn't used anymore. The lantern had been moved to the end of the west pier in 1881. We would have races to the end of the pier and back, Clara and me. Clara used to win 'til I turned twelve and grew these long legs of mine."

"Wow, it must have been really cool to live in a lighthouse!" exclaimed Lamar.

"Well, it was the only home Clara 'n me ever had, and we liked it though some folks said it was haunted."

"Haunted!!!" cried the whole class in unison.

"That's what I said… haunted. Do you want to hear about it?" Everyone nodded in agreement. Even Derrick became quiet as Mr. Davidson began his story.

"Well, there was a certain Mr. Cuyler Cook who was the keeper of the lighthouse until the summer of '85— 1885 that is. Mr. Cook was in the process of movin' out of the keeper's house and turning the job over to his assistant, Mr. Samuel Phillips, when the biggest nor'easter in 100 years blew into Rochester."

"What's a nor'easter?" interrupted Justina.

"Well, most of the storms in the U.S. move across the

28

country from west to east or from California to New York. A nor'easter is a storm that moves in the opposite direction. It comes from the Atlantic Ocean and is meaner than Mrs. Levine when you haven't done your homework."

"Now I understand," laughed Justina, and Mr. Davidson continued with his story.

"Well, this was in the days before 'lectricity, and the oil in the lantern at the end of the pier needed to be replenished. Now usually Mr. Phillips just walked to the end of the pier, but on that August day the pier couldn't even be seen. It was all under water. It looked as if the lantern was just bobbin' up and down out to sea, not attached to anything, like a balloon let loose into an angry December sky. But Mr. Phillips knew that he had to get the oil out to the lantern. You see Mr. Phillips took his job as the light keeper seriously, and he was determined to keep that ole lantern lit."

"Just then Mr. Cook suggested they take the rowboat out to the lantern. Mr. Cook would row and wait for his friend to tend to the light. Then he would row him back to shore. Not being able to think of a better plan, Mr. Phillips agreed. Just imagine the strength in Mr. Cook's arms as he rowed against the pounding waves out to the pier. Unfortunately, Mr. Cook and his rowboat were no match for Mother Nature that day."

"Mr. Phillips had just made it out of the boat and stumbled onto the lantern when the boat, and Mr. Cook with it, capsized under the next ferocious wave. Mr. Phillips spent the whole night just hanging onto the lantern and, I imagine, praying a whole lot too. He was

rescued the next morning when the storm was over. Mr. Cook's body and broken pieces of his boat washed ashore a week later. Mr. Phillips saw to it that his friend had a proper burial. Then he boxed the rest of Mr. Cook's belongings and mailed them to his brother out in Kalamazoo, Michigan."

"So whenever we heard a strange noise or couldn't find something we had just set down, we thought it was the ghost of Cuyler Cook still looking to take care of the lantern. Mama said that if it was Cuyler Cook's ghost at least he was a friendly ghost, and that must be so, 'cause we had good luck the whole time we lived in that lighthouse."

"Did you ever see his ghost?" questioned Maria.

"Don't be stupid!" Derrick said scornfully. "You can't see ghosts. You just hear them or feel a breeze or see something move by itself."

"No, young lady," said Mr. Davidson patiently. "We never did see Mr. Cook's ghost, or nobody else's for that matter, though there was some strange happenings from time to time. Why, I remember this one time when Clara's history book was missing for a week. She finally found it in plain sight right on the kitchen table open to the section on the Great Lakes. Mama said that Clara just wanted to get out of doing her history homework and hid the book herself, but me and Clara, we thought that Mr. Cuyler Cook was looking to see if his name was in that book.

"Another time, Clara and me were playing just outside the tower when we heard someone walking on the tower stairs. We thought it was our daddy, and we went to see what he was doing. Well sir, when we opened the tower door, there was nobody in sight. We slammed that tower door tight and ran straight into the house. There was both Mama and Daddy sitting at the kitchen table."

"Tell us another story about the ghost," said Reinaldo.

"Yeah," chimed in the rest of the class.

"Well, from time to time and every year in August, at just about the time Mr. Cook drowned, we'd hear these strange scratching noises that seemed to come from inside the tower walls. They sounded like this. Everyone jumped as Mr. Davidson ran his fingernails over the whole length of the chalkboard. Daddy said it was just a mouse trying to find its way out, but me and Clara, we knew it was Cuyler Cook trying to send us a message. Only trouble was we never could figure out what that message was s'posed to be."

"Enough talk of ghosts," said Mrs. Levine. "Tell us about the lighthouse today."

"Well, now that's a sad story, boys and girls. 'Cause modern ships have things like ship-to-shore radios, sonar and depth finders, lighthouses have become obsolete. That means we don't need them anymore. In fact the Charlotte keeper's house has not been lived in since 1982. That's before all of you were born. Now some friends and I would like to rebuild the lantern and make the lighthouse into a museum. That takes some money though, and money's the thing we just don't have."

"We could hold a bake sale," volunteered Debra.

"I appreciate the offer, but it would take about 1,000

bake sales to get enough money to do all the fixing we need."

"The Lighthouse Society has raised some money," volunteered Mrs. Levine, "but it still needs about $100,000 to restore the lighthouse and open it as a museum."

"That's right," continued Mr. Davidson. "With local factories making job cuts it's not so easy to get that kind of money."

Debra nodded as he said this. She knew only too well about job cuts. Her dad had just lost his job at Kodak, and he already had told her and her sister that the only place they would be going this summer was "Porchville." On that somber note the school day ended, and the kids escorted Mr. Davidson to his car. As he slowly drove off in his gray Buick Century, everyone resolved to help Mr. Davidson and the lighthouse in any way they could.

Chapter 7

The next day the study groups got together to brainstorm ways to help the lighthouse. The Sea Dragons (Group 1) decided to sell Popsicles at lunchtime and after school. They figured that if they bought the Popsicles in bulk and sold them for twenty-five cents each, they could make a profit of sixteen cents on every Popsicle. All they had to do was to get Mrs. Smith, the lunch lady, to lend them space in her freezer.

The Barnacles (Group 2) voted to try making and selling stone paperweights. They decided to collect smooth stones from the beach and get Mr. Nguyen the art teacher to help them turn the stones into ladybugs, beetles, and even people.

The Jellyfish (Group 4) wanted to get the whole school involved, and asked Mr. Coley, the principal, for permission to put a big jar to collect pennies in the front hall. They would go class to class and explain the project. Their slogan would be "Let The Lighthouse Live."

Janie and Jeanetta wanted to collect pop cans and bottles and return them to Wegmans for the deposit money. "My dad's already got a whole case of beer bottles we can have," volunteered Janie. The boys agreed that they could find as many, if not more, cans than the girls, and The STARfish's plan was put into action.

That afternoon Derrick, Lamar, and Reinaldo were walking home from school as usual when Lamar said, "Let's get together tonight and start collecting returnables. We'll find all the cans and bottles in the neighborhood before the girls even start looking." They agreed to meet at 7:00 P.M. in front of Lamar's house and each bring a half dozen plastic bags.

At 7:00 P.M. they set off with garbage bags hanging out of their pockets. Mrs. Green, Lamar's mother, waved to them from the top step. "You can put your full bags right here on the front porch. Stick together, and don't forget to say thank you."

Their first stop was right at the curb where someone had dropped a broken bottle and two dirty cans. They decided right away that they wouldn't pick up any broken bottles and would put all the dirty bottles and cans into one bag so that they could wash them later. Next door, Mr. Nelson let them have all the returnables he had, saying, "This will save me a trip to the recycling center." Between houses they checked out areas next to fences and under trees and came up with lots of dirty but usable containers. They even wrestled a can away from Mrs. Allen's dog Buddy.

By 8:15 P.M. there were four bags of clean returnables and three bags of dirty returnables on the Green's front porch. "Why don't you come in for some homemade apple pie?" said Mrs. Green.

"Ummm, apple pie," said Reinaldo, who never said no to food.

"That sounds great, Mama," said Lamar, "but can't we go out for just a little while longer? We haven't been down Arbutus Street yet."

"You know I don't like you out after dark, but this is for a good cause, and you're doing such a good job. I'll let you go out one more time, but you must be back by 9:00 P.M. at the latest. Take this flashlight with you and promise me you'll stay out of trouble."

"We promise," the three boys said in unison. Unfortunately, it was a promise they could not keep.

Chapter 8

The boys raced out the door again with the flashlight dangling from Lamar's belt. They had collected about a bag and a half of bottles and cans when it seemed like night fell all at once and everything turned dark. Then the wind became stronger. Derrick tripped over a heave in the sidewalk, and all three of them let out a shriek when something whooshed by them in a flash.

"Oh, it's only a cat chasing a leaf," said Lamar with relief.

After a few more steps Derrick said, "Look at that tree." Its branches were bowed down by the wind and almost touched the sidewalk. "It looks like a witch's fingers ready to snatch us up." All three boys started running past it at once.

Reinaldo swore he could hear a witch cackle as they flew past.

"Maybe we should go home now," he worried. "I'm ready for a piece of that apple pie."

"Let's just go a little longer and fill up this second bag," said Lamar.

"You're not worried about seeing a ghost are you?"

said Derrick.

"Of course not," replied Reinaldo. "I don't believe in ghosts."

"What about the ghost of Cuyler Cook at the light-house?" asked Lamar.

"Well, maybe there's a ghost living in that old light-house, but there aren't any ghosts here on Arbutus Street."

"That's right," said Derrick as he moved a little closer to his two friends.

A few minutes later, as they put the last bottles and cans into the bag, Derrick looked up and pointed across the street. "Look where we are. Isn't that the house where Janie lives?"

"It sure is," said Reinaldo. "I bet she's scared of ghosts."

"Wouldn't it be fun to find out?" asked Derrick.

"How are we going to do that?" said Lamar.

"Well, didn't Janie say that she lives upstairs and that her bedroom window faces the backyard? We could sneak back there and scratch on her window like the ghost of Cuyler Cook did at the lighthouse."

"What if Mr. Washburn catches us?" said Reinaldo. "He'll kill us."

"We'll leave our cans here so we can be real quiet," said Derrick. "Besides, she might not even be there."

The three boys tiptoed along the side of the Washburn's house and crawled once they got in the backyard. Looking up, they saw not one, but two, heads in Janie's bedroom window. "Oh, this is great," whispered Derrick. "Jeanetta's there too, and we can scare them both at once."

The girls had gotten together to do each other's hair and just hang out. Jeanetta loved combing Janie's fine, straight hair that was so different from her own. Janie liked trying to bead Jeanetta's coarse, kinky hair although the result was not quite the same as when Jeanetta's mom did it.

"How are we going to get up to the second floor, and what will we use to scratch the window?" said Reinaldo, getting more nervous by the minute. "Maybe we should just go home."

"It's easy," said Derrick. "We'll break a branch off of this maple tree here and use it for scratching. I'll climb up to that limb that's near the window, and you two can stay down here. If anyone comes, flash the flashlight one time and I'll come down."

Breaking the branch was easy, and Derrick stuck it through his belt loop as he began to climb. Lamar held his breath as he watched Derrick climb higher and higher. Reinaldo kept moving his eyes around the yard looking for adults and/or ghosts. Both boys were wishing they were back in the Green's kitchen. It wasn't long before Derrick had scaled the trunk of the tree and was crawling out on a branch near the top. Under his weight, the limb dipped to just above Janie's bedroom window. Then, leaning down as far as he could, Derrick took the branch out of his belt loop and began to scratch the window. Janie and Jeanetta didn't even look up. They were looking at a picture of Leonardo DiCaprio in a teen magazine while listening to a CD of *Titanic* music.

Scratch, scratch, scratch . . . .

They were oblivious to what was going on outside.

"Maybe you should come down now," said Lamar in a loud whisper.

"Let me reach farther and scratch louder," replied Derrick, who was determined not to give up.

The girls were still not paying attention when Derrick made one last lunge for the window. At the very moment that Derrick scratched loud enough to get the girls to turn and look, he lost his balance and started to fall. The girls looked out in time to see him grab ahold of the nearest object, which happened to be a rusty gutter pipe that was already breaking away from the house. Lamar and Reinaldo had just enough time to dive out of the way before Derrick and the gutter pipe came crashing to the ground. Reinaldo yelled, "We need to get out of here!" He and Lamar were halfway out of the yard when they looked back and realized that Derrick was not following them. With one look at each other they both turned and went back to help their fallen friend.

Chapter 9

"Are you OK, Derrick?"

"Did you get hurt, Derrick?"

The boys kicked away pieces of the broken gutter and each grabbed one of Derrick's arms in an attempt to get him off the ground.

"I think I'm OK," said Derrick as he managed to stand up. However, when he put weight on his left foot, it would not hold him; he collapsed again on the ground.

"Help me up again," he directed his friends. They stuck their arms under his and held on tighter this time. The three musketeers started hobbling out of the yard right into the path of Mr. Washburn, who had run out of the side door when he heard the crash. He grabbed all three of the boys by their jackets and glared at them with murder in his eyes.

All of a sudden out of the darkness came a loud "Help!" followed by the sound of falling returnables.

"Our bottles and cans!" yelled the three boys at once. Mr. Washburn relaxed his grip on them, and he and Lamar and Reinaldo rushed to the front of the house. Derrick slowly followed. There, in a pile of cans and bottles, with her glasses askew, sat old Mrs. Brady from next door. Dressed in bathrobe and slippers, she was still clutching a baseball bat, which she had grabbed for protection on the way out the door. She had been getting ready for bed when she heard the noise and went outside to investigate. Unfortunately Mrs. Brady's night vision did not match her courage and she stumbled over the bags of returnables in the dark.

The boys were afraid to speak as they helped Mrs. Brady out of the pile of cans. By this time the girls, as well as four or five more neighbors, had congregated on the Washburn's front lawn to see what all the commotion was about. "Derrick, Lamar, and Reinaldo, what are you doing here?" said Jeanetta.

"Are these your classmates, Janie?" quizzed Mr. Washburn. "I recognize Derrick from detention, but who are these other boys?"

"This is Lamar and that's Reinaldo. They're in my class, but I don't know what they're doing here, Dad. I didn't invite them. Honest. I didn't."

"I didn't invite them either," said Jeanetta. "Cross my heart and hope to die." She took her index finger and made a cross over her heart.

"I want to know what in tarnation those bags were doing in the middle of the lawn?" demanded Mrs. Brady as she adjusted her glasses and tied up her bathrobe. At that point Lamar and Reinaldo poked Derrick, who started to explain what happened.

"You see, Mr. Washburn, Lamar and Reinaldo and me, we were just trying to help out the lighthouse by looking for old cans and bottles. Janie must have told you about helping the lighthouse."

Mr. Washburn still had a skeptical look on his face and one hand on Derrick's shoulder. "I know all about the lighthouse project, Derrick. But don't you have any cans in your own neighborhood, and what made you climb the tree? You didn't really expect to find any cans in the tree, did you? I haven't seen any squirrels drinking Coke lately." He laughed at his own joke, but then scowled at Derrick again. "Don't you boys go anywhere either," he said to Reinaldo and Lamar, who had been quietly backing away.

"So, Derrick, tell me why you were in the tree."

Derrick looked at Reinaldo and Lamar, but they were both looking at the ground. He looked at Janie and Jeanetta. They were both staring at him with eyes wide open. Finally he looked back toward Mr. Washburn and spoke into his chest. "Well, we did collect cans in our own neighborhood, but we wanted to get some more. See, we wanted to collect more than the girls could. That's not wrong, is it?"

"The tree, Derrick. Why were you in the tree?"

"Well, when we saw Janie and Jeanetta in the window, we, I mean I, thought it would be kinda sorta fun to scare them. You know, to scratch on the window like Cuyler Cook's ghost scratches on the brick at the lighthouse. We were just playin'. We didn't mean to cause any trouble, did we guys?"

Mr. Washburn looked at Reinaldo and Lamar who were nodding in agreement.

"Now I think we're getting to the truth," said Mr. Washburn. He relaxed his grip on Derrick's shoulder.

"You should know better than to try to scare us, Derrick Davis," said Jeanetta.

"Yeah," said Janie.

"Well, since I'm not hurt I guess there's no harm done," said Mrs. Brady. "These old bones of mine must be stronger than I thought," she laughed.

"You're very kind, Mrs. Brady," said Mr. Washburn, "but I think these boys owe you something for your inconvenience. Why don't they come by next Saturday and do some yard work for you?"

"That would be dandy!" exclaimed Mrs. Brady. "Since the mister died it's been hard for me to take care of the house by myself. Besides it might give these boys something to think about besides ghosts," she added with a wink.

As Mr. Washburn walked Mrs. Brady back home, Lamar happened to look down and notice Derrick's foot. "Derrick, your ankle looks as big as a baseball."

"It does hurt," replied Derrick reluctantly. He was afraid to cause any more problems.

"Let me look at it," said Dr. Hoover, who lived across the street. He picked Derrick up and carried him to the front step.

"We'll help you clean up," offered Janie as Lamar and Reinaldo reached for the bag and started gathering cans and bottles again.

"You're not mad at us for trying to scare you?" asked Lamar.

"Well, you didn't do a very good job of it, and I think you got scared as much as we did," replied Janie. "And I bet Derrick's mother won't let him play outside for weeks."

"Oh, my gosh!" exclaimed Lamar looking at his watch. "I just remembered that we were supposed to be home by nine o'clock. It's so late. My mother's going to kill me!"

"I was going to call your mothers anyway," said Mr. Washburn who was back from seeing Mrs. Brady home. "Let's go inside. It looks like we're going to have to get Derrick's ankle x-rayed."

Derrick's mother called a neighbor to look after Louis and Richard and hurried over to take Derrick to the emergency room. As they were leaving, Mr. Washburn said, "I will expect all three of you over here as soon as Derrick's ankle is healed to help me replace that gutter. I hope you have learned a lesson. Derrick could have been killed in that fall, and if someone had called the police, you all could have been arrested for trespassing. Lamar and Reinaldo, you get in my car, and I'll drive you home."

Lamar's glasses did not work magic and keep him out of trouble that night. The Green household was not a happy place to be after he got home. Mrs. Green burst into tears when Mr. Washburn came to the door with Lamar. That made Lamar feel worse than he already felt, which was pretty bad. Then there was his father. Right now he was working the B-shift at Rochester Products, and Lamar was glad he'd be asleep by the time he got home.

Things were equally somber in the Santiago household. Both Mr. and Mrs. Santiago were waiting for Reinaldo with steam coming out of their ears. As soon as he stepped inside the door, they both let loose a string of Spanish words so loud and fast that Reinaldo could not understand half of them. He did, however, understand that they were angry. His parents seldom spoke Spanish anymore except when they were very angry or very happy, and Reinaldo knew that his parents were not happy.

Chapter 10

It was three subdued boys who showed up for school on Monday morning. The x-rays of Derrick's ankle had shown no broken bones, but rather just a bad sprain. The doctor's advice was to put ice on it, take Tylenol, and stay off of it as much as possible. Derrick wanted to stay home from school, but Mrs. Davis said, "What? And give you more time to get into trouble?" She borrowed some crutches from the Pelusios down the street and drove Derrick to school herself.

It was 8:25 A.M. when Derrick slid out of his mother's car. He started hobbling toward the school, using one of his crutches to push a rusted soup can out of the way. When Lamar spotted him, he ran over to take his book bag. Reinaldo, Janie, Jeanetta, and most of the other fourth grade students weren't far behind.

"Hey, watch it with those crutches!" yelled Janie as she fell into the chain-link fence that surrounded the school playground. "You tripped me."

"I can't help it if you're clumsy," said Derrick.

"Stop arguing, you two," said Tomas. "I want to hear what happened to Derrick."

By 8:35 the story of the bottles, the tree, the ghost, the girls, and Mrs. Brady had spread from the kindergarten all the way up to the sixth grade.

Mrs. Levine insisted on hearing the whole story, but her body seemed to droop downward as she listened to her five students each relate part of the tale. "I'd hate to think that something we learned about in this classroom caused such an incident to happen. Didn't you boys learn anything from your salvage attempt at the beach?" Then she proceeded to go on for another fifteen minutes about how they could have been killed and how it was terrible to attempt to scare the poor girls anyway.

Derrick was thinking about his theory that teachers got paid extra each time they gave kids a big lecture. There goes another $100 for Mrs. Levine, thought Derrick, but even he wasn't dumb enough to say it aloud.

"Don't you want to see how much money we made with the cans and bottles?" Lamar asked when Mrs. Levine paused to take a breath. He pulled an envelope from his back pocket and took out three ten-dollar bills. "The returns came to $27.95 and my mother added the rest of the money to make $30.00."

Mrs. Levine's eyes brightened just a little bit as she took the money and put it into a special jar the class had decorated to look like a lighthouse. "Well, at least something good came from this episode. We are now on our way to saving the lighthouse."

The week ended with their first trip to the lighthouse. After the episode at the library and the adventure in the tree, Mrs. Levine was reluctant to let Janie and Derrick go with the rest of the class. She wasn't sure if they would be able to stay out of trouble. Finally she compromised and let them go on the condition that their parents go along as chaperones. So on Friday at 8:45 A.M., Mrs. Levine, Mr. Washburn, Mrs. Davis, twenty students, and one pair of crutches boarded the Lake Avenue bus for their first trip to the lighthouse.

Mr. Davidson met them at the bus stop and escorted them the rest of the way up to the lighthouse. "As you can see we need to clear out this brush," he said as he held a drooping tree limb up so the group could pass under it. "By the way, did you all know that years and years ago the Native Americans used to put up their fishing tents on this property? I wonder what it looked like then."

"Maybe our class could help you with clearing that brush," said Mrs. Levine, looking at Derrick. "We have some boys who just love cutting tree branches."

"How come the lighthouse is so far from the water?" asked Janie.

"Where's the light?" blurted out Anthony.

"Remember I told you that the light was moved out to the end of the pier in 1881? For years deposits of dirt got carried down the Genesee River and built up the riverbank so that the light became too far inland. We'll walk out to the pier to see it when we're done with the house."

It wasn't hard to imagine a ghost living in this house. The concrete steps crumbled underneath them as the group filed carefully in. Once inside they noticed that some of the walls were brown where water coming in from holes in the roof had rotted the plaster. Parts of the

floor were so warped that it looked liked the funhouse at an amusement park.

"Be very careful boys and girls. I don't want anyone to get hurt," warned Mr. Davidson.

"Where did you sleep?" asked Maria.

"Where did you and Clara hear the ghost scratching?" asked Donald.

"Follow me and I'll take you upstairs to the bedrooms where we slept. Then we'll go into the tower where we heard the scratching."

The stairway railing had broken loose, but the stairs themselves were intact so they climbed one after another to the second floor. The upstairs was much like the downstairs, with stained walls and uneven floors. "You should have seen this place before we started cleaning up. The first thing we had to do was take power tools and uncover the windows, which had been covered up by concrete slabs. Try to imagine this place being totally dark."

Actually, the students had no trouble imagining this house in darkness. Mrs. Levine saw more than one student looking over his shoulder while Mr. Davidson was talking, and she knew they were looking for signs of a ghost.

Chapter 11

"Now, it will be very crowded when we go into the tower," explained Mr. Davidson as he led the group out of the house. It was just a couple of quick steps from the house to the tower. In fact they were so close that from a distance they looked like they were attached. "Some of you will have to sit on the window ledges. You can tell how thick the walls are by how wide the window seats are."

The tower was totally different from the house. The outside of the house was covered in smooth red brick. Even though it needed repair, it looked like a city house, straight and even and refined. The tower looked like its country cousin—the one who had been adopted into the family but didn't really fit. It was made from coarse, uneven, brown stones. The walls were over a foot thick, tilting inward so that they almost came to a point at the top. The space inside was small.

"This is like a dungeon," said Reinaldo.

"No, it's like a fort," said Lamar. "You could shoot guns out those windows."

"Wow! Look at those twisty stairs," exclaimed Tomas.

"Can we go up them?"

"Everyone can go up 'em but only one person at a time. After the light was removed the stairs were sealed with a board at the top so they don't actually lead anywhere. By the way, they are called spiral stairs. The original ones were built of wood in 1822, but they were replaced with these cast iron stairs in 1853. Back then things was made to last. By the way, does anyone know what shape this tower is?"

Everyone looked at Jeanetta, who was looking down. She thought for a minute, then said, "The floor has eight sides so the floor, itself, is an octagon, but I don't know what you call a tall building like this that has a larger octagon at the bottom and a smaller octagon at the top."

"You call it a lighthouse," said Derrick. Everyone laughed, and Mrs. Levine said, "You'll learn more about that in high school. Tell us more of the lighthouse history, Mr. Davidson."

So Mr. Davidson continued on telling lighthouse stories as one by one the group members quietly took turns winding up and then down the forty-two twisty stairs. When almost everyone had had a turn, Reinaldo called out, "What about Derrick?"

"Oh, I can hop up and down those stairs on one foot," proclaimed Derrick.

"Oh, no you can't," said Mrs. Davis and Mrs. Levine at the same time. "This is one part of the trip you'll have to miss," added his mother.

"Now can you show us where you heard the ghost scratching?" asked Anthony.

"Why, that's right over here," replied Mr. Davidson, pointing to a brick about two feet off the floor on the back wall of the tower. "If you're real quiet maybe Mr. Cuyler Cook will talk to us today."

Everyone stopped talking, some even tried to stop breathing, and the lighthouse became as silent as a school during summer vacation. They listened for one, then two, then three minutes, but there was no sound at all.

Eventually Mrs. Levine said, "I wish you boys and girls were this good at listening in the classroom. I'm afraid we'll have to wait for the ghost some other time. We have to head out to the pier now or we won't be back in time for our bus. It will take us at least ten minutes to walk out there and another ten minutes to walk back. On our way let's look for small rocks that The Barnacles can use for their paperweight project. But if you find a rock with a hole in the center or a black one with a thin white ring around it, you better keep it. Those are supposed to be lucky." The group filed out with some grumbling, but soon got caught up in looking for lucky stones.

At the end of the pier Mrs. Levine made everyone sit as Mr. Davidson gave another history lesson. "I get nervous with you all standing too close to the water," she said.

"The old lantern that was once on the top of the lighthouse sat on the end of this pier from 1884–1931," explained Mr. Davidson. "It was replaced in 1931 by this tower."

"What did ships do before the lighthouse was built?" asked Tawanda.

"Good question," replied Mr. Davidson. "Before the lighthouse was built people would hang lanterns on two butternut trees, one on each side of the harbor. They were called pilot trees."

"Can we see them now?" asked Donald.

"No. Unfortunately, both trees died and had to be cut down."

Derrick groaned. He didn't want to be reminded of falling trees.

Too soon it was time to go, and the group thanked Mr. Davidson and began hiking back to the bus stop.

"Oh no! I think I lost my watch," said Janie as they were almost there. "Can I go back and get it? The last time I saw it was when we were in the tower."

"Yes, if you can hurry," said Mrs. Levine.

Janie tore back up the hill toward the tower, scanning the ground as she went for any signs of a Snoopy watch with a bright yellow watchband. Just as she reached the door to the light she heard it. There was a scratching noise coming from inside. She tiptoed in and then stood perfectly still. The scratching got louder and was coming from the exact spot that Mr. Davidson had pointed out. Janie was frozen in place until the sounds of the kids calling her name broke the spell. All at once Janie remembered why she was there. She quickly searched the floor and found the watch under the first step of the spiral stairs. Grabbing it up with one hand she ran out the door and back down the hill. The class was already on the bus. Only her father was waiting outside.

"I heard the ghost! I heard the ghost!" Janie shouted

as she boarded the bus.

"No, you didn't," said Derrick.

"Did too."

"Not!"

"Too!"

"You go girlfriend!" shouted a voice from the port side of the bus, and everyone started to laugh.

Mrs. Levine stepped to the bow of the bus and let out her fourth sigh of the day. On a scale of one to ten this one was at least a seven. "I was really hoping that we could have a quiet ride home. Mrs. Davis, would you move up here next to Derrick, and Janie, would you and your father sit near the back? Maria, bring me my purse. I think I need some Tylenol."

Chapter 12

The next few weeks were calm but busy at school, as the groups worked on their fundraising projects. Opinion was just about equally divided as to whether or not Janie had actually heard the ghost. The girls tended to believe her, and the boys tended to think that she made it up. There was no doubt in Jeanetta's mind that it really happened since Janie "truced" her, and everyone knew that when you hooked your first two fingers up with your friend's first two fingers and "truced" you couldn't lie.

The second trip to the lighthouse was a working trip. Mr. Davidson wasn't sure that they were old enough to help with the physical work of cleaning up the lighthouse, but Mrs. Levine had assured him that they were very good at physical work. Armed with everything from paper towels and Windex to hedge clippers and rakes, Mrs. Levine's fourth grade class and chaperones once again boarded the Lake Avenue bus. This would be a whole day affair with Mr. Davidson and members of the Charlotte Lighthouse Society providing lunch and Kool-Aid breaks. Mr. Washburn, who had traded shifts at the firehouse to come along, supervised the outdoor group while Mrs. Davis led the indoor workers. Louis and Richard were home with Grandma.

Mrs. Davis swore that she would not let Derrick out of her sight, but when she started showing Justina and Debra how to strip off wallpaper, Derrick hobbled out the door and over to the tower. Mr. Washburn said that he would not take his eyes off Janie, but when he turned to help Bobby and Shekeya bag a bulky pile of chestnut tree branches, Janie sneaked over to the tower. She met Derrick at the tower door.

"I bet you're too scared to go in," taunted Derrick.

"I bet you're too scared to go in," countered Janie.

They stared at each other for a full minute. Then, without speaking, they both moved toward the door. The doorway was wide enough so that the two of them could cross over the threshold at the same time if they went shoulder to shoulder, which they did.

"It's too quiet in here," whispered Janie.

"Why are you whispering?" asked Derrick in a voice not much louder than Janie's.

"Because I don't want to wake up Cuyler Cook's ghost."

"I want to go up the twisty stairs," said Derrick, continuing to whisper.

"You know your mama doesn't want you to do that," said Janie. "Neither does Mrs. Levine."

"How are they going to find out? You're not going to tell them are you?"

"Well, no, but hurry up before we both get in trouble again."

Scratch, scratch, scratch . . . . .

Derrick threw down his crutches at the base of the stairs. He reached up for the railing and started hopping up the stairs on his good leg, one step at a time. Meanwhile Janie inched over to the brick where she had heard the scratching on their last trip. Derrick was over halfway up the stairs when the moaning started.

"Stop that Janie."

"Derrick, it's not me," said Janie, backing away from the tower wall.

"Janie, quit moaning. I know you're trying to scare me."

"DERRICK, IT'S NOT ME!" screamed Janie as the moaning got louder. "I'm going back out..."

BLAM! The tower door slammed shut. Derrick was so startled that he lost his balance. Before he knew what was happening, he started bouncing down twenty-seven of the forty-two stairs, scraping his back on the metal treads. In a matter of seconds, he landed in a heap on top of his crutches at the bottom of the stairs. He looked up at Janie, who was standing over him.

"HELP!" They both started to scream at once. Mr. Washburn was the first to reach the tower door and yanked it open. Janie ran into her father's arms, but he was not so willing to embrace her.

"What's going on in here? You two were screaming bloody murder. And what are you doing in here in the first place? Janie, you're supposed to be helping me outside, and Derrick, you're supposed to be helping your mother inside."

"I know, Dad, but..."

"Never mind. I don't want to know. Janie, you're

going to spend the rest of the day sitting on the bus. Derrick, I'm going to let your mother deal with you."

By this time, the rest of the students had come running and wanted to know what happened.

"We heard the ghost, and Janie got scared and started screaming," said Derrick.

"Liar! You were just as scared as I was."

"I wasn't scared. I screamed because I fell down the stairs and got hurt," said Derrick holding his back with one hand.

"Stairs?" said his mother who had just arrived at the door. "What were you doing on the stairs?"

"Janie wanted to see me hop up the stairs on one foot."

"Liar!" said Janie getting in his face.

"Go to the bus. Now," ordered her father, grabbing her by the shoulders and pointing her in the direction of the bus.

"Derrick, you come with me," said Mrs. Davis. "We'll talk about this some more when we get home."

"Liar!" shouted Janie one more time over her shoulder as she stomped off toward the bus.

Mrs. Levine was happy to stay back and let the parents handle this one. Once Janie and Derrick were taken care of, she tried to get the rest of the students back to work.

"Do you really think they saw Cuyler Cook's ghost?" asked Reinaldo.

"They didn't say they saw his ghost. They said they heard a ghost. That's two different things," said Jeanetta.

"You always think you're so smart," said Bobby.

Mrs. Levine let go another of her famous sighs (8 on

the scale). "Now children. It's bad enough we've got Janie and Derrick fighting. I don't want you to start fighting too. There's no such thing as ghosts, so they must have been imagining things. We know that Janie and Derrick both have big imaginations. Now, can we please get back to work? We've only got an hour left and lots more to do."

Reluctantly, the students resumed what they were doing before the interruption, quietly debating among themselves whether Janie and Derrick had heard a ghost or not. By the end of the day, forty-three bags of brush stood by the road waiting for the city to pick them up, and all of the old wallpaper had been removed from the bedrooms. Mrs. Davis saw to it that Derrick peeled one whole wall by himself. Mr. Davidson was very impressed.

"I bet you'll all be in bed early tonight," predicted Mrs. Levine as they boarded the bus. In fact, about half of the students fell asleep before the bus turned off of Lake Avenue, and Mrs. Levine started nodding off, herself. Janie and Derrick pouted in their separate corners. It was a sighless trip home.

Chapter 13

The children were not the only ones interested in restoring the lighthouse. The Charlotte Lighthouse Society held a formal dinner dance at the yacht club and raised $3,455. Holy Cross Catholic Church agreed to hold a yard sale and donated all of the $1,826 profits to the lighthouse. This money was used to buy shingles for a new roof. It was agreed that the roof should be fixed first so that any inside repairs would not be ruined by rain. With the help of nine neighborhood volunteers the new red roof was nailed down in only one week.

The Sea Dragons sold Popsicles every day at lunch and after school. At the end of one month, they had sold 872 Popsicles (blueberry was the biggest seller). At a profit of 16 cents per Popsicle, they had raised $139.52.

The Barnacles, with Mr. Nguyen's help, had transformed 79 plain rocks into 79 beautiful paperweights and had sold them at the #27 School Spring Festival (where it snowed) for $1.50 each. That gave them a profit of $118.50 since the rocks were free and Mr. Nguyen donated the paint.

The STARfish were forbidden to do any more door-to-door searches for bottles and cans, but they were allowed to put a box in the front hall of the school and at the local Wegmans grocery store for people to contribute. They made sure the returnables were cleaned and bagged. 2,347 bottles later, they had made $117.35. This, added to their previous $30.00 gave them $147.35.

The Jellyfish spent three hours rolling all of the coins that had been dropped in the jar in the front hall. The total came to $296.52. Rodney had volunteered his mother to take the rolled coins to the bank and exchange them for paper money. They were so heavy that they had to call Mr. Rivera, the custodian, to help carry them out to her car.

Mrs. Levine carefully wrote each group's name on the board with the amount collected by them next to it. "The first person who adds this correctly gets one of the leftover Popsicles," said Mrs. Levine.

"Can we use a calculator?" asked Janie.

"Janie, it will take you longer to punch in all of the numbers on your calculator than it will to add it mentally."

"I don't think so," mumbled Janie under her breath.

"I've got it!" shouted Jeanetta at the same time. "It's $701.89."

"See," said Mrs. Levine. "That wasn't so hard."

"Not for Jeanetta," mumbled Janie. Sometimes she thought that she might not like Jeanetta if she wasn't her best friend.

"I've got another Popsicle for the person who can tell me how much more money we need to make it $702 even."

"That's easy," said Reinaldo. "It's eleven cents."

Everyone stared at Reinaldo who was not known for his great math ability or his speed. Reinaldo just shrugged and said, "Hey, when food's involved my brain works pretty good."

Mrs. Levine laughed and said, "Now there's a person after my own heart."

Chapter 14

A few days later Mr. Davidson came by to pick up the hard-earned cash. He thanked the children over and over and said, "This money will sure buy lots of cans of paint. And, better still, the business owners in the Charlotte area have agreed to match your amount. You kids have set a great example for your parents and the other grownups. Because of your enthusiasm, we've been getting offers of help from everywhere. When Mr. Tubman from Tubman's Hardware Store heard about the project, he agreed to sell us anything we need at cost. Mr. Howard from the Lilac City Nursery donated grass seed and shrubs, so we're taking care of both the inside and the outside.

Work seemed to go on around the clock at the lighthouse. Mr. Davidson spent so much time there that he felt like he was the light keeper now. He didn't say so out loud, but he didn't mind that feeling at all. Actually, Mr. Davidson hadn't felt so important in a long time. Everyone was coming to him for decisions about what color to paint this and how to arrange that. The Lighthouse Society decided to restore part of the lighthouse as closely as possible to how it looked in the 1870s when the light was still in the tower. Of course Mr. Davidson wasn't even alive then, but his family had at least one picture, and the logs of the former keepers and the blueprints of the building were on file with the U.S. Coast Guard.

Before long the lighthouse looked better than new. The red bricks on the house had been cleaned and the holes patched with new mortar. So had the bricks on the tower. Every window was spotless and all the trim painted ivory. Leading up to the new stoop was a brand new sidewalk. On either side of the walk was a freshly trimmed lawn and some mulberry bushes. A new brass knocker hung on the new front door. The surrounding fence had been repaired and painted, and the black gate now latched securely.

The inside of the lighthouse had also been transformed. Although not historically correct, a small apartment with a modern kitchen had been built upstairs so that once again a caretaker could live in the lighthouse. The walls had been wallpapered in a pattern popular in the 1870s. The floors were carpeted and new lights added to show off the historical artifacts. The three downstairs rooms were now officially a museum.

The garage did not escape remodeling either. It was to become a space for special exhibits. The porch was transformed into a small gift shop. The only thing missing was the light. The $70,000 cost of a new cast iron lantern was more than the Lighthouse Society could afford even with all of their fundraisers. They, however, had not given up hope and continued to look for ways to get the money.

The only thing left to do was to plan a ribbon-cutting ceremony for the official reopening of the lighthouse as The Charlotte-Genesee Lighthouse Museum. The special event would take place on Saturday, May 8. Of course, Mayor Johnson would be the one to actually cut the ribbon, but Mrs. Levine's class had been invited as special guests. "I mustn't forget my friends who worked so hard for this day," said Mr. Davidson.

Most of the conversation now revolved around what to wear for this important event. After all, the *Rochester Democrat & Chronicle* would be there along with the three local TV stations and the R News cable station to take pictures and interview people. Jeanetta wanted everyone to get dressed up in their best clothes, but the boys would have none of that. Lamar wanted them to dress as pirates, but Mrs. Levine quickly vetoed that idea. She had visions of kids with eye patches accidentally goosing society ladies with their plastic swords.

"Even pretend weapons have no place at this event," she announced.

After lots more discussion, the class decided to wear their school T-shirts, which were yellow with black writing and a picture of a bumblebee (for Susan B. Anthony) on the upper left-hand corner. The PTA agreed to have each child's name embroidered under the bumblebee so that any adults would know to whom they were speaking. Parents agreed to provide black pants or shorts and white socks and sneakers to complete the uniform. School #27 students would certainly stand out in the crowd.

Like most teachers, Mrs. Levine was concerned about more than just their appearance.

"We have to act and sound smart as well as look smart," she said. "I want people to remember you for your intelligence and not just your T-shirts."

All week they did practice interviews with Mrs. Levine's big permanent marker serving as the pretend microphone.

"Remember, talk directly into the microphone and don't look at the ground. Answer questions with 'yes' and 'no,' not 'yeah' and 'no way dude.' And I shouldn't have to remind you to be polite."

They also reviewed the lighthouse history that Mr. Davidson had taught them so that they could enlighten any passerby who asked.

Derrick thought they should practice their handwriting since someone might want their autographs. He wasn't sure if he should sign just Derrick Davis or Derrick Davis of The STARfish. This started an argument, which gave Mrs. Levine the chance to give one of her sighs (only a 4).

"Derrick, this is not the NFL, and you're not Refrigerator Perry," she said. "If anyone asks for your autograph, I will personally carry you on my back up the forty-two twisty stairs at the lighthouse."

Chapter 15

May 8 finally arrived—60°, but gloomy and overcast, with rain in the forecast. Since it was Saturday, the kids were attending the festivities with their parents. They all agreed to meet by the triangular rose garden under the flags.

"Look for me," said Mrs. Levine. "I'll be wearing my #27 school T-shirt and will be the biggest bee buzzing in the lighthouse garden. Look for Mr. Levine, also. He'll be buzzing around in yellow, too."

By 1:45 P.M. nineteen of the students and about twenty-nine parents had arrived. Mrs. Levine was happy to see so many parents, since some kids, like Janie and Derrick, lived in single parent homes, and other kids' parents had to work or keep previous commitments. At 1:46 P.M. Reinaldo came running up to complete the group. His parents trailed behind, pushing baby Maria in the stroller.

"She almost made us late," said Reinaldo while pointing at the curly-haired baby with the big brown eyes. Maria seemed unconcerned as she kicked her legs and bounced up and down.

"Don't worry," said Mrs. Levine. "The ceremony

doesn't start until 2:00 P.M., and Mayor Johnson is not here yet. We will have time to walk over to the lighthouse slowly like ladies and gentlemen." She barely got the word gentlemen out when Donald started sprinting away. He was followed closely by Derrick, who was moving much too fast for someone who had only recently been able to give up his crutches.

"I think it's going to be a long afternoon," whispered Mrs. Levine to her husband as they both took off after the children.

The lawn of the lighthouse and the path leading up to it were getting more crowded by the minute as more people arrived for the ribbon cutting. The children were having a hard time staying together as a group, and some had convinced their parents to take a walk out to the pier while they were waiting.

"Great! Now I've lost the parents as well as the students," moaned Mrs. Levine. Meanwhile, a bearded man wearing brown cords, a black T-shirt, and a big Kodak camera hung around his neck seemed to be eavesdropping on some of the students.

"What's that you said about a ghost living in the lighthouse?" he asked.

Jeanetta spoke for the group in her best classroom voice. "Mr. Davidson visited our classroom and told us about a ghost who lived in the lighthouse when he was little." She went on to explain all about Cuyler Cook, his accidental death, and the scratchings in the wall. She concluded by saying, "and my best friend Janie Washburn has even heard the scratching herself." This was followed by a chorus of boys trying to convince him that it was just a lie.

"Can you show me exactly where you heard the scratchings, Janie?" asked the photographer. He told them that his name was Ron and that he worked for the *Democrat & Chronicle*.

"Sure!" replied Janie as she led him in the direction of the tower.

Mr. and Mrs. Levine had gone looking for scattered students and parents, and didn't notice The STARfish following Janie and Ron to the tower. As they walked, Derrick mumbled to the other boys, "Now watch. Janie will get her picture in the paper for doing nothing."

Once inside the tower, Janie led everyone to the back wall. "There it is!" she exclaimed as she pointed to the brick that was two feet off the floor. They all watched silently as Janie knelt down in front of the wall. The scratching began just as she touched the brick, and no one was more surprised than Janie.

"That's it! That's it!" she shouted as she drew back her hand in fear.

Reinaldo started for the door, but Derrick strode right up to the protruding brick and grabbed it. "I'm not afraid of any ghost!" he said. As he spoke, a big chunk of mortar fell out and the brick started to pull away from the wall. Not only did the scratching continue, it seemed to be getting louder.

"I'm not either," said Janie as she grabbed the other side of the brick. She had gathered her courage and was not about to let some boy outdo her.

"Now look what you've done," said Reinaldo from the spot where he had stopped half in and half out of the doorway. "You've broken the lighthouse and we'll all be in trouble again."

Ron, who had been snapping pictures, pushed his camera aside and stepped closer. "Let me see what's going on here," he said. He reached out with both hands and grabbed the brick just as Derrick and Janie, who were wrestling for control, were about to drop it. Setting the brick carefully on the floor, Ron reached into the opening and felt around.

"I think a few more of these bricks are loose," he said. "The workmen must have missed this spot when they repaired the cracks."

While the others watched, Ron, Derrick, and Janie took out three more bricks and lots of pieces of loose mortar. Janie reached into the enlarged hole one more time and this time touched something different. "There's something else back here, and it feels like metal."

"Take it out," said Ron, Jeanetta, Lamar, and Derrick in unison.

"No, the ghost will get mad," protested Reinaldo from his post at the door. "Come on. The mayor's here, and Mrs. Levine is looking for us."

"Let me help," said Ron. He took his jackknife out of his pocket and used the blade to pry the metal object loose and wiggle it out of the wall. "This Swiss Army Knife comes in handy for the darndest things," he said as he triumphantly held up what looked like a rusted old metal box.

"It doesn't look very exciting," said Lamar.

"Open it up," said Derrick, who had not given up on the idea of lost treasure.

"Has anybody else noticed that the scratching stopped as soon as Ron took the box from the wall?" asked Jeanetta.

Everyone paused to listen, and Jeanetta was right. The tower now was silent except for human noises.

Chapter 16

"I'd love to open this box, but it's locked," said Ron.

"Use your knife to get it open," suggested Derrick.

"I probably could, but maybe we should let Mr. Davidson know about this first."

"Oh, oh! Here's Mrs. Levine and she doesn't look happy," moaned Reinaldo, who was now trying to hide behind Ron.

"I was wondering where you had all disappeared to," scolded Mrs. Levine in her meanest teacher voice. "Don't you know that Mayor Johnson is here and is speaking right now? Even your parents didn't know where you were. I swear I'm going to have to tie you all up to the..." Mrs. Levine stopped speaking as she looked up and saw Ron. "Oh, I didn't know you were with someone from the press," she said as she smoothed out her hair and straightened her glasses. "Still, you should have told someone where you were going."

"This might be all my fault," said Ron as he walked toward Mrs. Levine with his hand extended. "I'm Ron Van Hall from the *Rochester Democrat & Chronicle*, and you must be Mrs. Levine."

"Yes I am," replied Mrs. Levine as she put out her hand to meet Ron's. "Have these children been bothering you?"

"Not at all. My question about a possible ghost led us to a curious discovery." Ron explained the sequence of events and finally held up the rusty green metal box. "We were about to show this to Mr. Davidson when you arrived. Don't you agree that he should be the one to open it?"

"Why yes, but I can't imagine that there's anything valuable inside," said Mrs. Levine, whose frigid look had thawed to the slush stage.

Ron handed the box to Janie, and The STARfish immediately started running back to the front gate where Mayor Johnson was just opening the scissors and beginning to cut the ribbon.

"Wait!" yelled Derrick. "We have something to show you."

All eyes were on Janie as she handed the recovered box to Mayor Johnson. "What's this?" he asked as he set the scissors aside and began turning the box over to examine it. Then he handed it to Mr. Davidson, who shook it and turned it over again.

Ron, who had returned to snapping pictures, stepped forward to explain the whole situation again. However, Derrick, who had seen the television cameras rolling, jumped in front of him and began relating his version of the story. No one was going to get between Derrick and a television camera. When he was finished, Mr. Davidson agreed that the box should be opened immediately, and he borrowed Ron's knife to do the job.

"I just know there's money in there," said Derrick. "I heard it clang against the box when it rolled over."

"It doesn't take a genius to figure that out," said Janie. "What else would you find in a box like this?"

"Actually, there's a pile of stuff in here," said Mr. Davidson as he broke the lock and pried open the cover. "Look at this. It's a watch with initials and what looks like a date engraved on the back. Let's see. The initials look like CEC and the date looks like 1876.

"Oh!" exclaimed Jeanetta. "That must've belonged to Cuyler Cook. His initials would begin and end with 'C.'"

"You betcha, little girl," said Mr. Davidson. "He's the only light keeper we've had with those initials, and his middle name was Eugene."

"Is the watch running?" asked Debra.

"Don't be dumb," said Derrick scornfully. "A watch that old couldn't be running. The battery would be dead."

"Nope. It's not running," said Mr. Davidson. "But it's not 'cause it needs a new battery. Watches back then didn't have batteries. They ran by winding the moving gears. Maybe we could get this watch running again if we tried."

"I guess Debra's not the only dumb person here," said Janie as she glared at Derrick. However, Derrick wasn't paying attention. He wanted to know what else was in the box.

"What about money?" he asked.

"Well, there is some money here."

"I knew it!" said Derrick.

"Hold out your hand while I count out these old bills.

They're pretty faded, but I think we can still make out what they are. Ten, twenty, thirty, forty," he began. "Fifty, sixty, seventy…one hundred twenty, one hundred twenty-five, one hundred thirty, one hundred thirty-one, one hundred thirty-two, one hundred thirty-three, one hundred thirty-four dollars even. That was lots of money back in them days. I bet this was government money. Years ago lighthouse keepers also had to collect custom duties, money that foreign ships had to pay when they came into American ports. Mr. Cook was probably safe-keeping money he had collected from Canadian ships entering the port of Rochester.

Derrick looked disappointed. "You sure there's not more money in there, and are you sure that what is there belongs to the government?"

"Well, there are some coins in here that look like silver dollars."

"Maybe there're worth more today," said Derrick, not wanting to give up.

"Let me see those," said Mr. Moran, a member of the Lighthouse Society. "I'm interested in old coins, and maybe I could figure out how much they're worth."

"Are you sure there's not anything more?" whined Derrick.

"Give it up," said Lamar. "It looks like our treasure chest turned out to be a sunken chest."

"You can look for yourselves," said Mr. Davidson. "All that's left is this here piece of wrinkled paper. It's got some printing on it, but I can't quite make out the words. Janie, your eyes are better'n mine. Can you read any of them?"

"I think I see the word 'dry,' and there's some other letters that look like 'p' and 'a' and 't'. And there's a number here that looks like a '10.'"

"I'll take a look at that," offered Mr. Levine, who was a lawyer. "Perhaps I can figure out what it says."

"If anyone can figure it out, it will be you, dear," said Mrs. Levine, smiling at her husband.

"Let's get back to the ceremony and officially open this museum," said Mayor Johnson as he reached for the scissors. With one neat cut the ribbon was slit, and the event was recorded for posterity and the evening news. The crowd started to disperse—some for the inside of the museum to have their first glimpse of the remodeled lighthouse and some to the refreshment area for some cake and lemonade. The cakes were made in the shape of lighthouses, of course, twenty-two of them to accommodate all the people and to commemorate the year the lighthouse was built—1822.

The STARfish were disappointed at the contents of the "treasure" box, but they brightened up very quickly when they found out that they were going to appear both on the evening news and in the Sunday morning paper. Ron carefully took down all of their names so they would be spelled correctly.

Chapter 17

In school on Monday morning, everyone seemed to be carrying copies of the lighthouse story from the Sunday paper. Mrs. Levine allowed the class to read the story aloud over and over. Everyone kidded Janie about her arm being famous because the newspaper picture showed Mayor Johnson and Mr. Davidson, both with big smiles, receiving the metal box from Janie, or actually, from Janie's hand and forearm. The picture had been cropped at her elbow. Nonetheless, she was asked by the first graders to autograph the picture of her hand.

Then the debate started again about the ghost. All of The STARfish, now having heard the scratchings, were believers. "I know Cuyler Cook's ghost was trying to tell us where to find the box," said Derrick. "Why else would the scratching have stopped just as we got the box out of the wall? I just can't believe that he didn't have a fortune in gold coins stashed away."

"Aw, it was just some little mouse scratching," said Bobby. "My dad says there's no such thing as ghosts."

"Well," said Mrs. Levine, "about the ghost. I personally don't believe in ghosts. The truth is that we'll never know for sure what caused the scratching noise, so we're each free to believe what we choose." Nobody said anything, although Mrs. Levine saw a few students exchanging looks. She took advantage of the silence to press on. "Now, you all did a marvelous job helping to restore the lighthouse, but I think it's about time to get back to our schoolwork. We've been neglecting our lessons for quite awhile now. Open your math books to page 165, and let's work on long division."

Everyone groaned but slowly took out their books and turned to the designated page. In fact, with their heads in their books, the class almost didn't notice the appearance of Mr. Levine at the door.

"What are you doing here?" asked Mrs. Levine.

"Now don't worry, dear," he said calmly. "I have some good news, and I had to come right over and share it with you and the children. Remember that old piece of paper that was found in the box at the lighthouse? I had a hunch that it wasn't worthless, and I've been on the phone all morning long trying to find out more about it."

"Was it Confederate money?" asked Derrick. He was still convinced there was big money hidden in the lighthouse.

"Better than that, Derrick"

Derrick didn't think there was anything better than money, but he decided not to express that opinion, and Mr. Levine continued. "Janie thought she saw the word 'dry,' the letters 'p', 'a' and 't' and the number '10'. I used a magnifying glass to get a better look and found that the letters 'p', 'a,' and 't' were actually part of the word 'plate.'"

"There are some other words that are barely visible and legible only with the magnifying glass. The whole thing says 'Eastman Dry Plate and Film Company.'"

"Ohmigod!" exclaimed Mrs. Levine. She had just figured out the importance of the old paper.

"I still don't get it," said Jeanetta. If Jeanetta didn't get something, then nobody got it. "And what does the number '10' have to do with it?"

"Eastman Dry Plate and Film Company was the name of George Eastman's first company. He must have sold shares in it, and Cuyler Cook must have bought 10 shares," explained Mrs. Levine.

"That's right, dear. I did some research this morning and found out that the Eastman Dry Plate and Film Company was capitalized at $200,000 in 1884. Cuyler Cook was one of the first investors. He must have used his life savings to buy that stock."

"Oh!" shouted Jeanetta. "I get it. George Eastman was a famous Rochesterian, and the Eastman Dry Plate and Film Company is now what we call Eastman Kodak."

"How'd you figure that out?" Janie wanted to know.

"Easy. It was the word film. I just thought about who makes film and that's Kodak. Rain goes with Rochester like film goes with Kodak."

"Or Fuji," yelled someone from the back of the room.

"Bite your tongue," said Mr. Levine. "We don't talk about Fuji in Rochester."

"Wait!" interrupted Derrick. "I still don't know why

this paper is better than money."

"That's because it can be traded for money. Lots of money. I did some more phoning this morning and found out that with all the splits the stock has made this piece of paper is worth more money than Cuyler Cook could have stuffed in that green box, even if it were filled with $1,000 bills."

"Who gets the money?" asked Reinaldo, who had just become very interested in the discussion.

"I looked into that, too," replied Mr. Levine.

"My, you have had a busy day," said Mrs. Levine.

Mr. Levine just smiled and continued the explanation. "Cuyler Cook's name was on the certificate so the money should go to him. Since he's dead, it belongs to his surviving relatives. Mr. Cook died without having children but he had a brother. I called Michigan where his brother lived to find out about his family. The only remaining relative is a great-great-great-niece named Brenda Robinson who lives in the Sunny Hill Nursing Home in Kalamazoo. I spoke to Miss Robinson myself. She would like some of the money for her care at the nursing home, but she wants the rest of it to be used to finish restoring the lighthouse. She thinks that would be the best tribute to her great-great-great-uncle Cuyler. Of course, a plaque with his name on it will be hung in the lighthouse. Miss Robinson would also like to reward this class by buying you a state of the art computer system, software, and printers, and by throwing you a big party." Mr. Levine's last words were almost drowned out by the sound of twenty children and one teacher yelling, "Whooo!" as loudly as they could.

"Wait 'til Mr. Davidson hears about this," said Lamar.

"And don't forget Ron," added Jeanetta.

"I think I better take a computer class over the summer," mumbled Mrs. Levine under her breath.

Chapter 18

So that's how it happened that a month later Mrs. Levine's fourth grade class from Susan B. Anthony School #27 made its fourth trip to the Charlotte-Genesee Lighthouse. A new Fresnel lens had been ordered from Cleveland, and the lantern had been made in cast iron. Both were hoisted to the top of the tower by an Army crane. Finally the lighthouse looked exactly like it did in 1875. Tomorrow would be another grand re-opening of the lighthouse to the public, but today was a special preview for Mrs. Levine's class, their parents, and invited guests. The class had elected to have their party at the lighthouse, so this was to be an all-day affair with parent volunteers barbequing chicken, boiling potatoes for potato salad, and stirring up blue Jell-O with gummy fish. Mayor Johnson was there along with Mr. Davidson, Ron the photographer, and Mr. Coley, the school principal.

Ron, as expected, took plenty of pictures, and this time the Sunday paper featured a picture of all of The STARfish. Derrick was holding the green box. Janie was holding the old crumbled stock certificate. Lamar, Jeanetta, and Reinaldo were each holding bricks that looked like the ones from the lighthouse. The original ones had been securely cemented back in place. The headline in the paper that day said "STARFISH STAR IN LIGHTHOUSE RESCUE." A framed copy with all five signatures was put on display with other restoration pictures in the lighthouse.

Mrs. Levine kept her word and carried Derrick on her back up all of the forty-two twisty stairs. Everyone applauded when they made it to the top and she set Derrick on the last step. He then climbed the ladder into the light, yelled to everyone forty feet below, and ran all the way back down. Mrs. Levine sat at the top of the stairs for twenty minutes catching her breath and finally staggered down the stairs, clinging to the railing.

A video of the whole restoration was made to send to Miss Robinson at the Sunny Hill Nursing Home in Kalamazoo and also to sell for $14.95 in the museum gift shop.

Mr. Davidson was appointed first curator of the new Charlotte-Genesee Lighthouse Museum and moved into the remodeled upstairs apartment. He said it felt wonderful to be back home.

Mr. Coley announced that since the new computer system, software, and printers had been given to Mrs. Levine and her class, it would only be right to keep them all together next year to enjoy the gift. Therefore, Mrs. Levine would now be teaching fifth grade at Susan B. Anthony School #27. Derrick noticed a tear fall from Mrs. Levine's eye. He went over to give her a hug when he thought that no one was looking.

The scratching noise in the lighthouse was never heard again.

Author's Note

The Charlotte-Genesee Lighthouse is a real structure standing at the mouth of the Genesee River where it empties into Lake Ontario in Rochester, New York. Dating from 1822, it has been lovingly restored in stages. Charlotte High School students were instrumental in its preservation. On Feb. 15, 1991, the U.S. government turned the property over to New York's County of Monroe which in turn gave a twenty-year lease to the Charlotte-Genesee Lighthouse Historical Society to operate it as a museum. Cuyler Cook was an actual lightkeeper who died in the manner described, although the year was 1853, not 1885. He did not leave behind any Eastman Kodak stock. William A. Johnson, Jr. was the sixty-fourth mayor of Rochester and its first African-American mayor. He served the city with distinction from 1994 – 2005. Everyone else in the story is fictitious.

References

de Zafra, Dorothea M. *Charlotte's Lighthouse and its River—How They Came to Be.* Rochester, NY: Charlotte-Genesee Lighthouse Historical Society, 1993.

Gateley, Susan Peterson. *Mirages, Monsters, Myths, and Mysteries of Lake Ontario.* Wolcott, NY: Whiskey Hill Press, 2001.

Harris, Bill. *Lighthouses of America.* New York: Crescent Books, 1991.

Ratigan, William. *Great Lakes Shipwrecks & Survivals.* Grand Rapids, MI: Wm. B. Eerdmans Publishing Company, 1960.

Rosenberg-Naparsteck, Ruth. *A Young Peoples' History of Rochester.* Rochester, NY: Corn Hill Navigation, 1990.

About the Author

Sally Valentine is a native Rochesterian, who has been both a student and a teacher in the Rochester City School District. After teaching math for 25 years, she is now off on a tangent of writing. She was inspired to write The Ghost of the Charlotte Lighthouse by her love for kids, books, and Rochester. When not writing, she can be found reading, solving puzzles of all kinds, scrapbooking, or walking around beautiful western New York. She lives in Walworth, NY with her husband, Gary. Her adult daughters and her granddog live nearby.